# Phoebe the Photographer:
## Gets A Camera

Copyright © 2016 Beryl Ayn Young
Illustrations by Darya Schegoleva
All rights reserved.

# Phoebe The Photographer Companion Guide
# Now Available Online!

Get the whole family involved behind the lens. Book questions for discussion + plenty of photography tips, tools, resources, and more!

http://www.berylaynyoung.com/phoebe/

*For Brielle & Bella - my bright lights*

If there was one thing Phoebe loved to do more than anything in the world, it was to laugh.

She laughed while collecting rocks.

She laughed when painting with watercolors.

She laughed when splashing in rain puddles.

She laughed when eating her favorite food, chocolate chip pancakes, for breakfast.

And, she laughed the loudest when she played with her best friend in the whole wide world, Lamby.

Phoebe's mommy and daddy loved telling her that laughing was her superpower, because her giggles could light up a room faster than the flip of a light switch.

"You're our bright light," her mommy shined.
"You're our happiness hero," her daddy beamed.
Phoebe liked being a superhero. It excited her how easily she could shine happiness with a smile and a laugh.

In fact, last week she saved the day while at the store with her mommy.

She tossed the grouchy, frowning checkout lady one convincing gleam of her sparkling, smiling eyes and instantly her grouchiness melted away.

That lady even shared an unexpected toothy grin and a wink with Phoebe before they left.

Phoebe took her job as a happiness hero seriously.
So seriously that on her 5th birthday, she wanted nothing more than her very own "Bright Light" superhero outfit.
The same one she saw last week at the grouchy checkout lady store.

It had a sunshiny gleaming yellow satin cape, a magenta sequin star on the back, a matching pink mask to block out darkness and evil, and gold glitter cuffs that had the power to stream light out of her wrists.

Phoebe knew that with that cape, she'd finally be ready to sprinkle her magic all over the world.

On Phoebe's special day, she opened gifts at the same time each and every year - precisely 4:08pm, the exact minute she was born. This year, Phoebe eagerly awaited the clock turning the magic hour when the fun would begin.

When it finally arrived, Phoebe tucked Lamby under one arm, spread both arms out like a bird soaring in the summer sun, placed a sparkly grin on her face, and zoomed down the stairs, just like a superhero ready to conquer the world.

And then, there it was!
Sitting in the middle of the kitchen table, was her pile of gifts. She ripped her way through the first five, and then at the bottom of the pile, she found exactly what she was looking for.

The present she was waiting for, all wrapped up in pink glitter paper, and tied off with sunshiny yellow ribbon.

"Happy birthday, Sunny Girl," her mom grinned.
"Are you ready for your beautiful day?" her dad smiled.

Phoebe anxiously tore open the paper while silently practicing her best superhero lines inside her mind.

"I'm Bright Light! My smile can brighten the darkest of villains faster than 1000 sunbeams! My laughter will melt the coldest of hearts!"

But when the paper was on the floor in shreds, something else sat in the place where her satin cape should've been.

A camera.

Phoebe frowned. She furrowed her brows. Crossed her arms. And glared like the evilest of villains at the box.

"This is for you to remember all your adventures," her mommy glimmered.
"You're going to love taking pictures. Why don't you go snap some now?" her daddy glowed.

Phoebe grabbed the box and her Lamby, turned her back on her parents, and moped back to her room.

Phoebe flopped on her bed and sighed.
"How will I ever be a superhero now?" she pouted to her friend.

She was frustrated.
"It's heavy, there are too many buttons, and it's not even yellow!" she exclaimed.

Phoebe turned the black box around in her hands as she turned her eyes towards the rays of afternoon light streaming in through the window.

She lifted the camera up to her eyes and curiously peered through the viewfinder. She liked what she saw, so her fingers searched for the shutter button and she pressed.

There on the screen were the most beautiful, shimmering rays of sunlight she had ever seen.

"Bright Light!" she whispered as she grabbed Lamby and ran off to chase the sun.

She hurried out the back door, shouting to her mom and dad as she left. "I'll be back! I'm going to use my camera now."

Using the sun as her guide, she skipped around the back yard, camera bobbing by her side, her best friend clutched tightly in her hands.

With each skip, she saw how the sun played peek-a-boo through the full tree branches and noticed how it was changing form - colors shifting from a bright white to gold. Sometimes showing its rays in big bursts, then retreating back into small streams of light.

'Click.'

She squinted one eye towards the trees,
raising her camera towards the other, and found a beautiful ray of yellow and orange streaming through a branch of summer leaves.

"Who needs a cape? I have the power to make the sun glow!"
she proclaimed as she grabbed Lamby and raced to
the top of the jungle gym.

She imagined they had soared up to the sky, dancing in the clouds,
twisting back and forth, watching the darkness and light dance
beside them.

Phoebe liked how the light made Lamby's fur shimmer and shine.

"Smile, we're about to save the day!" she sang as she snapped a photo of her trusty sidekick.

'Click.'

They whooshed down the slide and raced around the yard, clicking photo after photo of the beauty surrounding them, until Phoebe spotted the grumpy old lady, Mrs. Prickle, from next door. She was tending to her garden with a scowl.

"Mrs. Prickle, you look as beautiful as your flowers!" Phoebe beamed.

Mrs. Prickle turned towards her and cracked a small smile.

'Click.'

"My job here is done," Phoebe announced, scooping Lamby up into her arms, skipping away, then whirling and twirling around in circles, laughing and giggling until they both got so dizzy they floated like flower petals down to the soft grass.

Gripping her camera tightly, Phoebe turned to look into Lamby's beady black button eyes while capturing her threaded grin peeking through the flecks of long green grass.

'Click.'

Phoebe turned her gaze back at the sky, and let out a huge belly laugh.

She noticed the sky twinkling back at her with a magical sea of pinks, oranges, purples, and blues.

"Oh Lamby, look! We ARE superheroes. We made the sky smile," Phoebe exclaimed, standing up tall and proudly snapping image after image of the beautiful display of color and light.

'Click.'

'Click.'

'Click.'

As the sun began setting, they skipped back into the house.

"Welcome home, honey! Did you have fun?" her mom asked.
"We almost forgot, there's one last gift for you!" her dad announced.

Phoebe turned her eyes towards the table.

There, shimmering beautifully, was a long yellow satin camera strap with a line of magenta glitter stars running down the center.

"Bright Light to the rescue!" Phoebe proclaimed.

The smiles and laughter flowed as her mommy and daddy attached the strap to Phoebe's camera, and they all oohed and ahhhhed over her light-filled pictures.

On what had become the best birthday ever, Phoebe proudly holstered her glimmering camera over one side, and pranced up the stairs to bed.

Phoebe knew she WAS a superhero, and that her adventures were only just beginning.

## About Beryl

Beryl Ayn Young lives in Northern Virginia with her amazing husband, spunky daughter, two scaredy cats, and one high energy dog. In 2009 she became a professional photographer, by chance, after using a camera to heal after the profound loss of her first daughter during her 20th week of pregnancy. In addition to writing children's books, she teaches and mentors families how to love their photos and their life. Beryl believes that we're all superheroes in our own way; we just have to be willing to follow the light and uncover the truth of what makes each of us shine.

Learn more at **www.berylaynyoung.com**

Made in the USA
Las Vegas, NV
07 November 2024